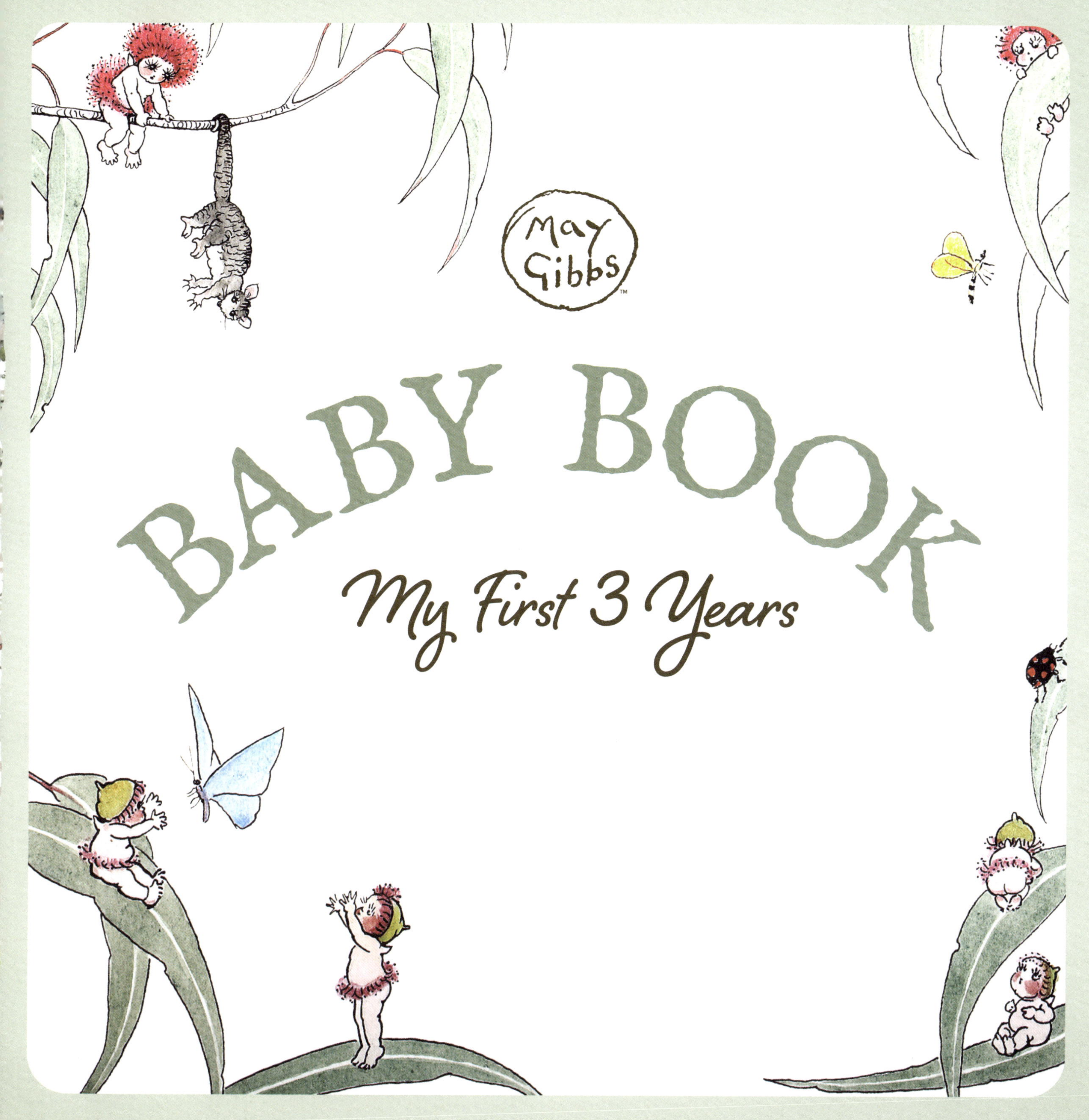
May Gibbs™
BABY BOOK
My First 3 Years

## A NOTE FOR FAMILIES:

This book is for mums and dads, and for caregivers and families of all kinds. Take your pen and make the book just right for your precious baby!



Published by Scholastic Australia in 2024.

Scholastic Australia Pty Limited
PO Box 579 Gosford NSW 2250
ABN 11 000 614 577
www.scholastic.com.au

Part of the Scholastic Group
Sydney • Auckland • New York • Toronto • London • Mexico City
New Delhi • Hong Kong • Buenos Aires • Puerto Rico

Designed by Stephanie Olive
Edited by Charlotte Bachali



ISBN 978-1-76129-084-8

Printed in China.

Scholastic Australia's policy, in association with its printers, is to use papers that are renewable and made efficiently from wood grown in responsibly managed forests, so as to minimise its environmental footprint.

*My name is*

_______________________________

# All about my Parents

THEIR NAME IS ______________________________

THEY WERE __________ YEARS OLD WHEN I WAS BORN.

THEY ARE SPECIAL BECAUSE: ______________________________

______________________________

______________________________

*Photo of my parent*

THEIR NAME IS ______________________________

THEY WERE __________ YEARS OLD WHEN I WAS BORN.

THEY ARE SPECIAL BECAUSE: ______________________________

______________________________

______________________________

OTHER MEMBERS OF MY FAMILY ARE ______________________________

______________________________

# Waiting for Me to Arrive

MY PARENTS FIRST FOUND OUT ABOUT ME ON ____________

MY DUE DATE WAS ______________________________

THIS IS HOW MY PARENTS TOLD MY FAMILY ABOUT ME:

____________________________________________

____________________________________________

MY PARENTS FIRST HEARD MY HEARTBEAT ON ____________

MY PARENTS FIRST FELT ME KICK ON ____________________

OOF! I was strong!

MY PARENTS' HOPES AND DREAMS FOR MY FUTURE:

____________________________________________

____________________________________________

____________________________________________

____________________________________________

____________________________________________

____________________________________________

*Ultrasound photo*

MY SCANS SHOWED:

- [ ] I WAS A BOY
- [ ] I WAS A GIRL
- [ ] MY PARENTS WANTED TO BE SURPRISED

HERE ARE A FEW NAMES MY PARENTS THOUGHT OF FOR ME:

______________________________

______________________________

______________________________

THEY DECIDED TO NAME ME ______________________ BECAUSE

______________________________

______________________________

My Baby
Shower

Shower invitation or photo

# Guest and Gift list

Guest: ______________________ Gift: ______________________

Guest: ______________________ Gift: ______________________

Guest: ______________________ Gift: ______________________

Guest: ______________________ Gift: ______________________

Guest: ______________________ Gift: ______________________

Guest: ______________________ Gift: ______________________

Guest: ______________________ Gift: ______________________

Guest: ______________________ Gift: ______________________

Guest: ______________________ Gift: ______________________

Guest: ______________________ Gift: ______________________

Guest: ______________________ Gift: ______________________

Guest: ______________________ Gift: ______________________

Guest: ______________________ Gift: ______________________

Guest: ______________________ Gift: ______________________

Guest: ______________________ Gift: ______________________

Guest: ______________________ Gift: ______________________

Guest: ______________________ Gift: ______________________

# My First Home

MY FIRST ADDRESS WAS ______________________

________________________________________

________________________________________

*Photo of our house*

# *I Love my Room!*

IT WAS DECORATED ______________________

______________________

______________________

*Photo of the nursery*

# I'm Here!

*The first photo of me*

I WAS BORN ON ________________ AT _________ AM / PM.

I WAS ☐ EARLY ☐ ON TIME ☐ LATE.

I WEIGHED ________________ KILOGRAMS.

I WAS ____________________ CENTIMETRES LONG.

I WAS BORN AT ____________________________________________

MY DOCTOR WAS ________________________________________

MY EYES WERE __________________________________________

MY HAIR WAS ___________________________________________

*Hospital bracelet*

MY BIRTH STORY: _______________________________________

# What the World Was Like when I was Born

THE PRIME MINISTER WAS ______________________________

FAMOUS MOVIES WERE ______________________________

POPULAR SONGS WERE ______________________________

A CUP OF COFFEE COST ______________ A LITRE OF MILK COST ______________

HERE ARE SOME NEWS HEADLINES FROM MY FIRST YEAR

# Little Me!

HERE'S MY HANDPRINT

HERE'S MY FOOTPRINT

LOOK HOW TINY I AM IN THIS PHOTO!

# My Firsts

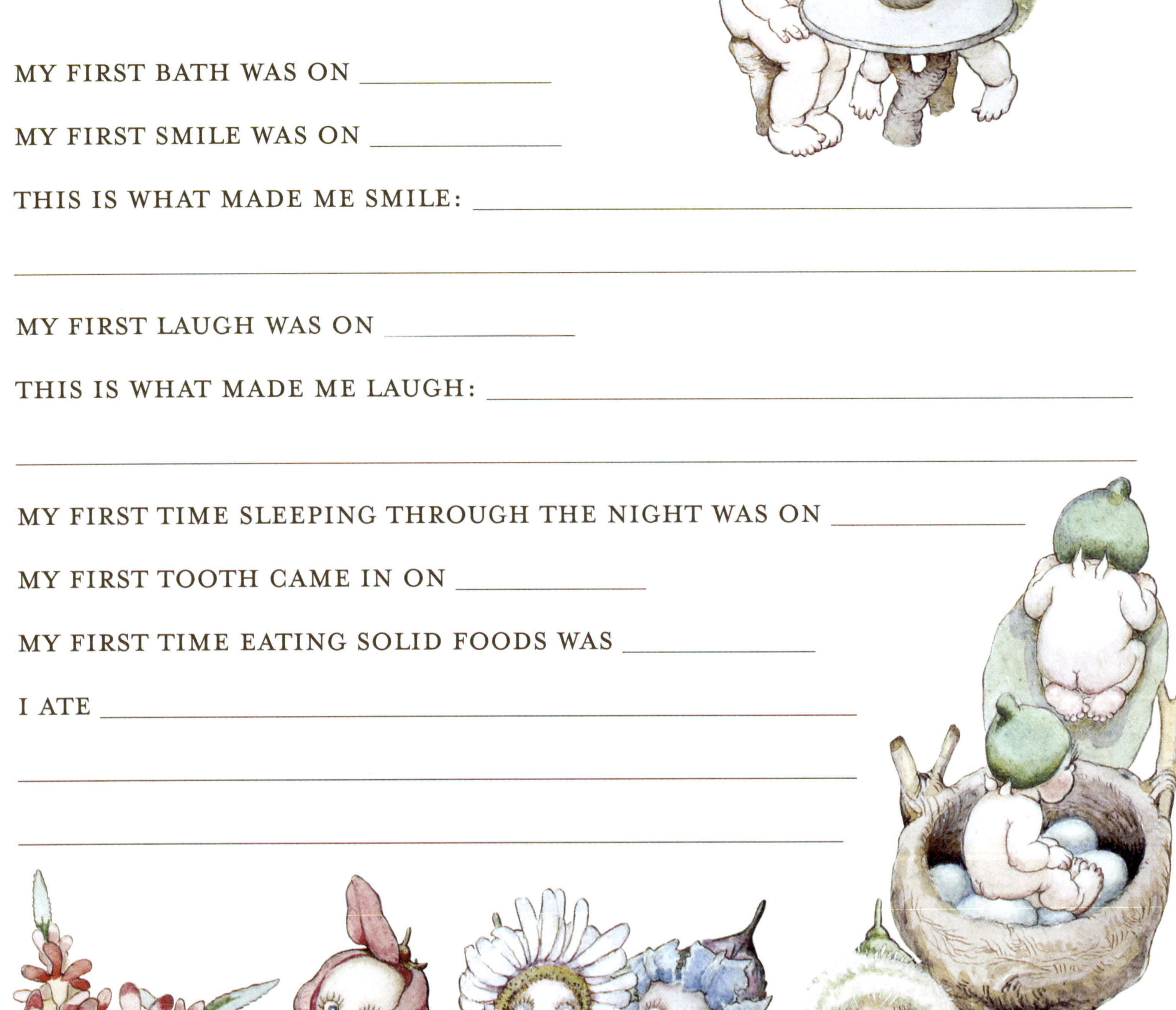

MY FIRST BATH WAS ON ______________

MY FIRST SMILE WAS ON ______________

THIS IS WHAT MADE ME SMILE: ______________________________________________

______________________________________________________________________

MY FIRST LAUGH WAS ON ______________

THIS IS WHAT MADE ME LAUGH: ______________________________________________

______________________________________________________________________

MY FIRST TIME SLEEPING THROUGH THE NIGHT WAS ON ______________

MY FIRST TOOTH CAME IN ON ______________

MY FIRST TIME EATING SOLID FOODS WAS ______________

I ATE ______________________________________________________

______________________________________________________________

______________________________________________________________

MY FIRST TIME CRAWLING WAS ON ________________

MY FIRST WORD WAS ______________________________

I SAID THIS ON ___________________________________

MY FIRST STEPS WERE ON _________________________

MY FIRST HAIRCUT WAS ON ________________________

*Photo of my first holiday celebration*

THE FIRST HOLIDAY I CELEBRATED WAS ____________________________________

# My 1ST Month

I WEIGHED ____________________ KGS.

I WAS ________________________ CM LONG.

SOME THINGS I LIKED TO DO: ____________________________________________

__________________________________________________________________________

__________________________________________________________________________

____________________________________________

____________________________________________

SOME THINGS I DIDN'T LIKE VERY MUCH:

____________________________________________

____________________________________________

____________________________________________

____________________________________________

*Photo at 1 month old*

Photos

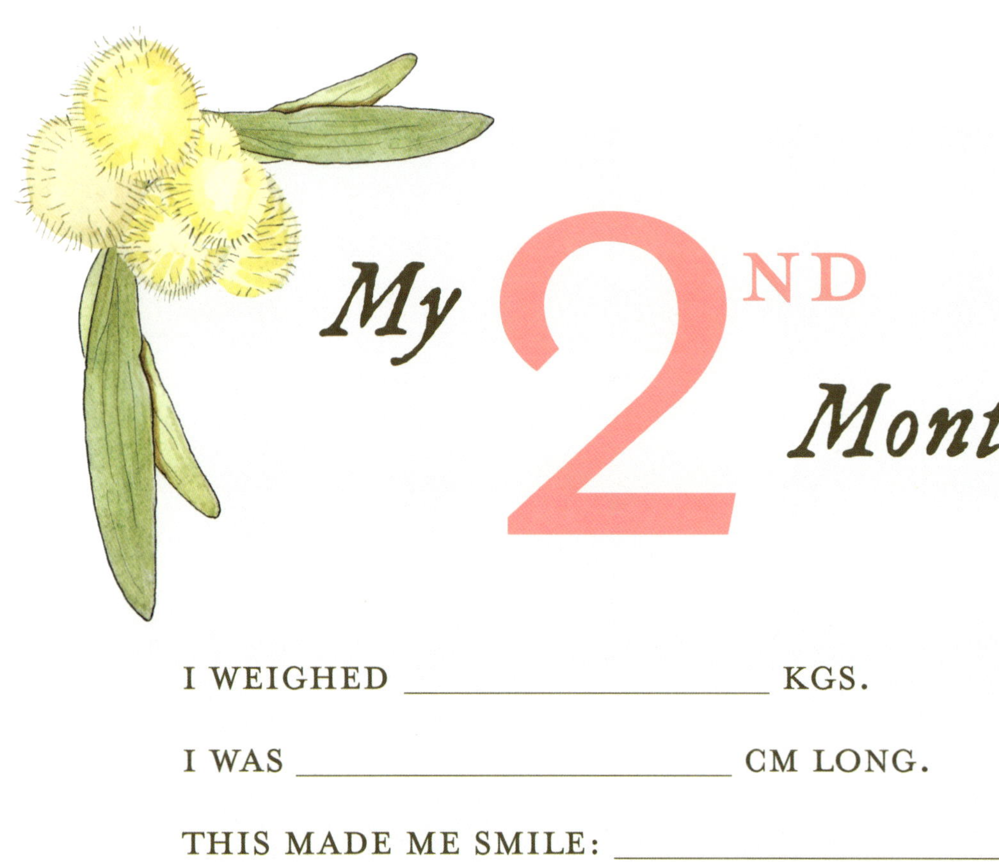

# My 2ND Month

I WEIGHED ____________ KGS.

I WAS ____________ CM LONG.

THIS MADE ME SMILE: ____________

THIS MADE ME CRY: ____________

Photo at
2 months old

Photos

# My 3RD Month

I WEIGHED ______________ KGS.

I WAS ______________ CM LONG.

SOME THINGS I DISCOVERED THIS MONTH: ______________

______________

______________

______________

Isn't that amazing?

OUR FAVOURITE PLACES TO EXPLORE WERE:

______________

______________

______________

Photo at
3 months old

Photos

# My 4TH Month

I WEIGHED ______________ KGS.

I WAS ______________ CM LONG.

THIS MADE ME HAPPY: ______________

______________

______________

THIS MADE ME GROUCHY: ______________

______________

______________

MY FAVOURITE TOYS WERE: ______________

______________

______________

______________

*Photo at 4 months old*

Photos

# My 5TH Month

I WEIGHED ______________ KGS.

I WAS ______________ CM LONG.

I WAS FASCINATED BY: ______________

______________

______________

______________

HERE'S WHAT I THOUGHT WAS SCARY:

______________

______________

______________

______________

______________

*Photo at 5 months old*

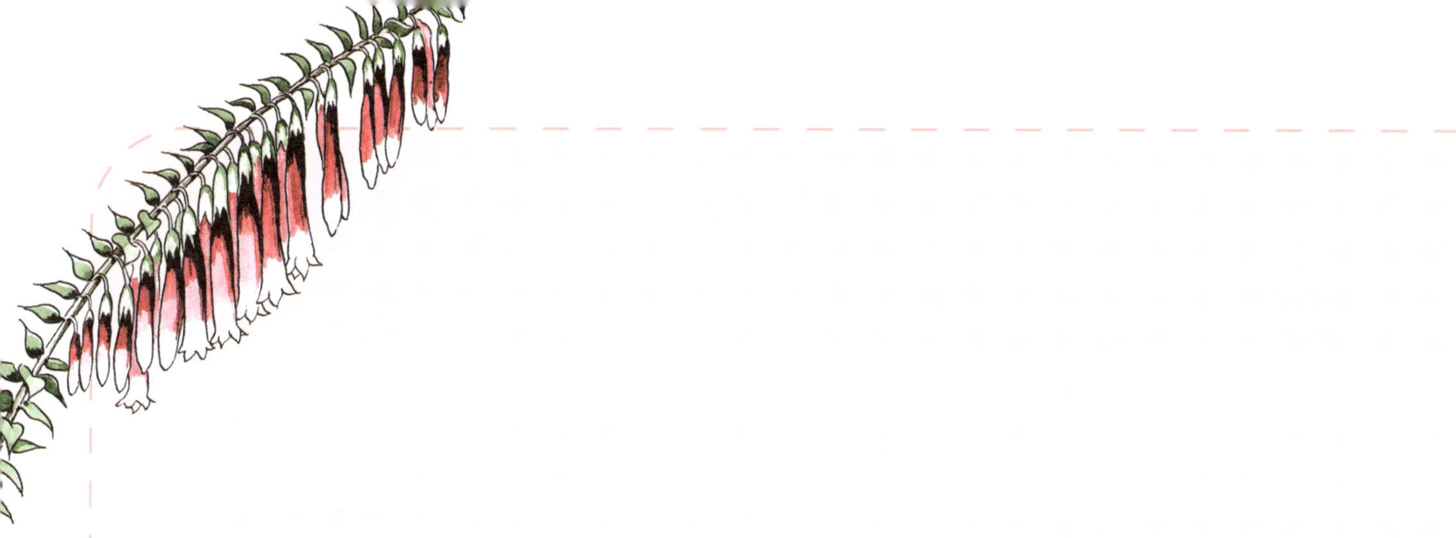

Photos

# My 6TH Month

I WEIGHED ____________________ KGS.

I WAS ________________________ CM LONG.

MY FAVOURITE FOOD WAS: ________________________________________________

______________________________________________________________________________

______________________________________________________________________________

Yum, yum!

BUT I DID NOT LIKE THE TASTE OF:

____________________________________________

____________________________________________

____________________________________________

____________________________________________

YUCK!

Photo at
6 months old

Photos

# My 7TH Month

I WEIGHED ________________ KGS.

I WAS ________________ CM LONG.

THINGS I LEARNT THIS MONTH: ________________

SOME PEOPLE I MET:

WOW!

(They thought I was adorable!)

*Photo at 7 months old*

Photos

# My 8TH Month

I WEIGHED ______________ KGS.

I WAS ______________ CM LONG.

MY FAVOURITE ACTIVITY WAS: ______________________________

______________________________

______________________________

______________________________

MY FAVOURITE BOOKS WERE: ______________

______________________________

______________________________

______________________________

______________________________

______________________________

*Photo at 8 months old*

Photos

# My 9TH Month

I WEIGHED ____________________ KGS.

I WAS ________________________ CM LONG.

I LOVED MUSIC, LIKE ______________________________________________________

__________________________________________________________________________

__________________________________________________________________________

____________________________________________

WHEN I HEARD IT, I WOULD _______________

____________________________________________

____________________________________________

____________________________________________

____________________________________________

____________________________________________

*Photo at 9 months old*

Photos

# My 10TH Month

I WEIGHED ____________________ KGS.

I WAS ________________________ CM LONG.

SOME SOUNDS I MADE WERE: ____________________________________________

________________________________________________________________________

MY FRIENDS WERE: ____________________________________________________

____________________________________________

____________________________________________

THIS IS WHAT WE LIKED TO PLAY: _________

____________________________________________

____________________________________________

____________________________________________

We had fun together!

Photo at
10 months old

Photos

# My 11TH Month

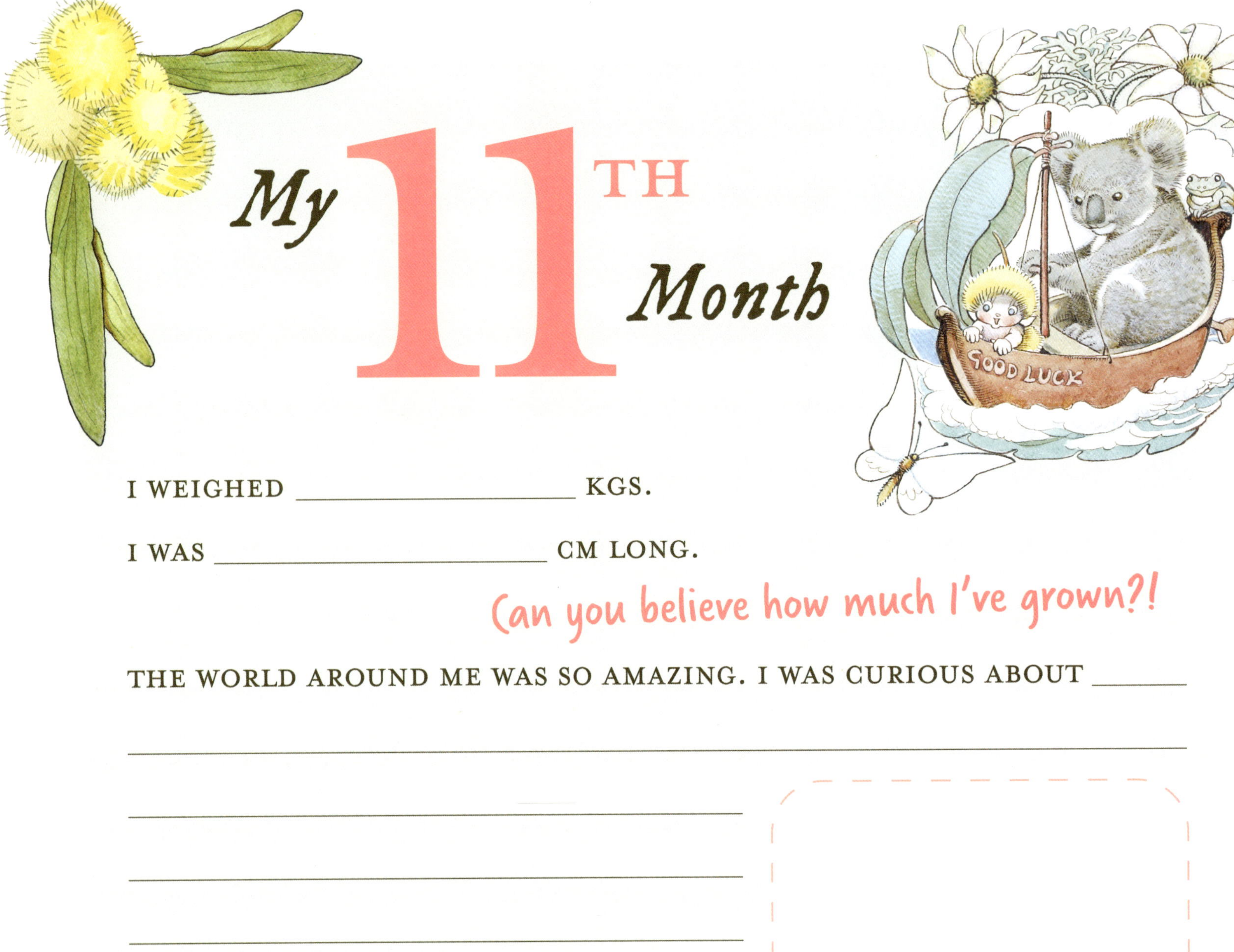


I WEIGHED ____________________ KGS.

I WAS ________________________ CM LONG.

Can you believe how much I've grown?!

THE WORLD AROUND ME WAS SO AMAZING. I WAS CURIOUS ABOUT ______

______________________________________________

______________________________

______________________________

______________________________

I THOUGHT IT WAS HILARIOUS WHEN _____

______________________________

______________________________

______________________________

Photo at
11 months old

Photos

# My 12TH Month

I WEIGHED ____________________ KGS.

I WAS ________________________ CM LONG.

SOME WORDS I SAID WERE: ________________________________________________

____________________________________________________________________________

HERE ARE SOME PLACES I VISITED: ________________________________________

____________________________________________

____________________________________________

____________________________________________

MY FAVOURITE OUTING WAS: _______

____________________________________________

____________________________________________

____________________________________________

*Photo at 12 months old*

Photos

# My First Birthday!

*First birthday photo*

LOOK HOW HAPPY WE WERE!

HERE'S WHAT WE DID FOR MY BIRTHDAY: ____________________

____________________

HERE'S WHO WAS THERE: ____________________

____________________

MY BIRTHDAY CAKE WAS ____________________

# Two Years Old!

Second birthday photo

LOOK HOW BIG I'M GETTING!

I WEIGHED ____________ KGS. I WAS ____________ CM TALL.

HERE'S WHAT WE DID FOR MY BIRTHDAY: ____________

____________

MY BIRTHDAY CAKE WAS ____________

AT TWO, MY FAVOURITE THING TO DO WAS: ____________

# Three
## Years Old!

*Third birthday photo*

THIS WAS SO MUCH FUN!

I WEIGHED ______________ KGS. I WAS ______________ CM TALL.

HERE'S HOW WE CELEBRATED MY BIRTHDAY: ______________

MY BIRTHDAY CAKE WAS ______________

MY FAVOURITE THINGS IN THE WHOLE WIDE WORLD WERE: ______________

______________

# How I Changed

| Year One | Year Two | Year Three |
| --- | --- | --- |
| FAVOURITE FOOD | FAVOURITE FOOD | FAVOURITE FOOD |
| FAVOURITE TOY | FAVOURITE TOY | FAVOURITE TOY |
| FAVOURITE PLACE | FAVOURITE PLACE | FAVOURITE PLACE |
| FAVOURITE SONG | FAVOURITE SONG | FAVOURITE SONG |
| FAVOURITE BOOK | FAVOURITE BOOK | FAVOURITE BOOK |

# Getting Creative

Year One

MY FIRST SCRIBBLE!

# Wonderful Me!

## Year Two

HERE'S A PICTURE I DREW OF MYSELF

AND HERE IS A PHOTO OF WHAT I LOOKED LIKE

# My Fantastic Family

I AM SO LUCKY TO BE PART OF THIS FAMILY!
HERE'S A PICTURE I DREW OF US

## Year Three

AND HERE IS A PHOTO OF
WHAT WE LOOKED LIKE